To Edward, Suzie, Rennie,
Victoria, Jay and Treacle – G.A.

For Hugo, with all my love – V.C.

ORCHARD BOOKS
338 Euston Road, London NW1 3BH
Orchard Books Australia
Level 17/207 Kent Street, Sydney, NSW 2000
First published in 2002 by Orchard Books
First published in paperback in 2003
ISBN 978 1 84121 290 6

A CIP catalogue record for this book is available from the British Library.
10 9 8 7
Printed in Singapore
Orchard Books is a division of Hachette Children's Books,
an Hachette Livre UK company.

The Magic Donkey Ride

Written by
Giles Andreae

Illustrated by
Vanessa Cabban

ORCHARD BOOKS

Treacle was a donkey
With a coat of golden brown,
And he lived beside a river
On a farm just out of town.

A little boy called Flinny
Was Treacle's closest friend,
And he loved to go and ride on him
For many hours on end.

Now, the funny thing with Treacle
Which perplexed poor Farmer Jack,
Was he never let the farmer
Take the saddle off his back.

When Flinn went down to see him
Farmer Jack would always say,
"I wish that he would let us
Take that saddle off one day!"

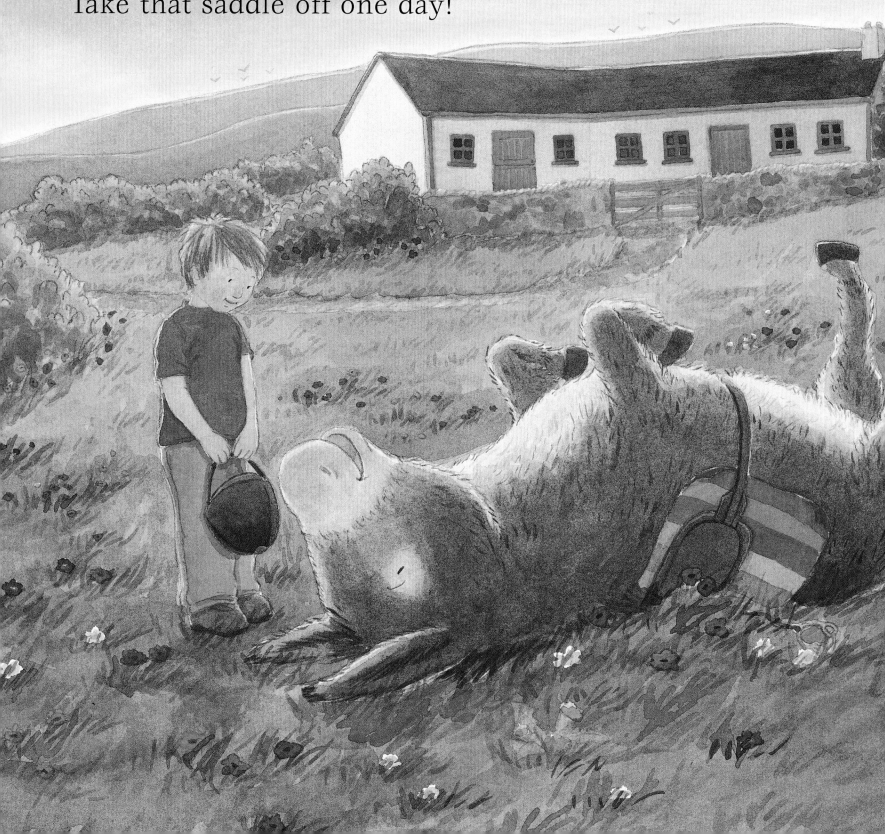

There's something strange about it
You can see it in his eyes."
Then something funny happened
Which took Flinny by surprise.

Treacle nudged his elbow
Then he winked at him and said,
"Meet me here at midnight
When the farmer's gone to bed!"

Flinn was so excited
That he didn't sleep at all.
The kitchen clock struck midnight
So he tiptoed down the hall.

Then he rushed across the valley
And he waded through the stream.
The starlight glittered brightly
Like starlight in a dream.

He ran into the meadow
And he came to Treacle's side.
Treacle said, "I'm going to take you
On a magic donkey ride!

Please take off my saddle
It's the heaviest of things."

"I don't believe it!" Flinny shouted,
"Treacle, YOU'VE GOT WINGS!"

"I know," said Treacle, smiling,
"No one knows they're there but you.
Now if you climb up on my back
I'll show you what they do!"

Then Treacle stretched his wings out
And he looked up at the sky,
"Let's go!" he shouted merrily
And they began to fly.

The warm night breeze
rushed past him
And his cheeks
began to glow.

Flinn looked down
from Treacle's back
And saw the
farm below.

The fields, as they
flew higher
Sparkled brightly
with the dew,

Then streams and meadows,
hills and towns
Came looming
into view.

"This truly is fantastic!"
Flinny shouted with delight.
"What a magic donkey ride!
WHAT A MAGIC NIGHT!"

Then Treacle landed softly
And he turned to Flinn to say,
"I only keep that saddle on
To hide my wings away.

So let's keep this a secret,
Don't let anybody know."
Then Treacle kissed him gently
And said, "Now you'd better go!"

So Flinn put back his saddle
And he patted Treacle's head.

Then, long before the morning,

He was fast asleep in bed.